Galen
AND Goliath

KidWitness Tales

KidWitness
T·A·L·E·S

Galen
AND Goliath

LEE RODDY

BETHANYHOUSE
MINNEAPOLIS, MINNESOTA

Galen and Goliath, by Lee Roddy
Copyright © 2001 by Focus on the Family
All rights reserved. International copyright secured.

Cover illustration by Chris Ellison
Cover design by Lookout Design Group

This story is a work of fiction. With the exception of recognized historical figures, the characters are the product of the author's imagination. Any resemblance to any person, living or dead, is coincidental.

A Focus on the Family book
Published by Bethany House Publishers
A Ministry of Bethany Fellowship International
11400 Hampshire Avenue South
Bloomington, Minnesota 55438
www.bethanyhouse.com

Printed in the United States of America by
Bethany Press International, Bloomington, Minnesota 55438

Library of Congress Cataloging-in-Publication Data

Roddy, Lee, 1921–
    Galen and Goliath / by Lee Roddy
        p.   cm. — (KidWitness tales)
    Summary: Ten-year-old Galen, an orphan boy who aspires to be a soldier in the Philistine army and carry Goliath's shield into battle, becomes friends with a young Israelite and learns about his God.
    ISBN 1-56179-955-6
    1. Goliath (Biblical giant)—Juvenile fiction. [1. Goliath (Biblical giant)—Fiction. 2. Philistines—Fiction. 3. Bible O.T.—History of Biblical events—Fiction. 4. Jews—Palestine—History—To 70 A.D.—Fiction. 5. Orphans—Fiction.] I. Title: Galen and Goliath. II. Title. III. Series.
    PZ7.R6 Gal 2001
    [Fic]—dc21   00-012432

1 2 3 4 5 6 7 8 9 10 11 12 13 14 15 / 08 07 06 05 04 03 02 01

To Jim Miller,

Fifth-grade teacher at Forest Lake Christian School,

Auburn, California

LEE RODDY's first short stories were published when he was 14. After committing his life to Christ, he moved to Hollywood and earned his college degree before beginning a professional writing career. Among his numerous publishing credits are 52 juvenile and adult novels and 15 nonfiction books, as well as award-winning television programs and films. Lee lives in California with his wife, Cicely. They have two grown children and two grandsons.

CHAPTER 1

Panting hard and ignoring the shouted insults of the watching Philistine soldiers, 10-year-old Galen quickly raised his small round shield. It blocked the blow from the tree branch that Leander thrust at him. Instantly, Galen struck with his own branch, catching the older, heavier boy high on the chest above his shield.

A wild cheer of approval from the boys on Galen's team mingled with groans of those supporting Leander. The soldiers shouted encouragement to both boys as Leander landed a strong counterblow to Galen's arm just above where he gripped his branch.

Galen winced, but the pain was nothing compared to what he had suffered at the recent unexpected deaths of his parents and only brother.

Leander's muddy brown eyes glittered with joy.

He puffed, "I told you that you'll never beat me! So quit before I have to hurt you!"

"No!" The word erupted from between Galen's clenched teeth. "You're bigger, but I'm going to carry Goliath's shield!"

Leander laughed nastily and feinted a thrust toward Galen's face. As Galen ducked behind his shield, he heard his adversary growl, "I'm already doing that, and no little lizard like you will ever take it from me! Now, this is your last chance! Quit now!"

Galen didn't reply, but in his frustration and pain he knew that his only hope for any future required him to give a strong account of himself in this elimination round of mock battle. He opened his mouth wide, yelled loudly, and began wildly slashing with his branch as he rushed upon his adversary.

This was so unexpected that Leander took two quick steps backward and tripped over his own feet. He fell to the sand. Derisive laughter erupted from the men, and Galen's friends shouted joyously.

Panting, Galen stood over his fallen foe. "Give up?"

"No!" Leander quickly swung his right leg up to hook his foot behind Galen's left knee. With a quick pull of his foot, Leander forced Galen's knee to buckle. He dropped heavily to the sand. Leander promptly kicked away Galen's shield and branch, then jumped onto his chest.

This brought roars of approval and loud applause from the soldiers, but Galen's friends groaned in unison.

The older, heavier boy leaned forward and thrust his dark face close to Galen's. Through clenched teeth, Leander hissed, "If you're ever going to be a big enough Philistine to carry Goliath's shield, you've got to win, no matter what! That's what I do—while you lose!" Leander's crushing weight kept him from replying.

Galen was aware of a sudden silence from the spectators. A shadow fell across Galen. He squinted against the sun as Leander leaped to his feet and stood at attention.

Galen's light brown eyes focused on the shadow maker. "Goliath!" the boy whispered, surging upright at the sight of the giant who stood more than nine feet tall.

Even though Galen had performed menial chores for Goliath, the boy was always overwhelmed at the sight of the Philistine army's greatest warrior. He wore a bronze helmet with the distinctive feather-like crown that made him look twice as tall as Galen. Goliath wore his 125-pound coat of mail and bronze greaves on his legs as if they were light as the desert air.

His deep voice mocked, "An ant tries to fell a bear." He laughed, a great booming sound of power.

Galen knew that if he was ever going to become the giant's shield bearer, he should offer some defense for his unfortunate position. Yet he couldn't think of what to say.

Goliath's mocking continued, "Galen the *healer* fights Leander the *lion-man*, and this is what happens."

Leander drew himself up proudly and threw out his chest at the giant's praise. Galen wished the ground would open up and swallow him before he was further humiliated.

Goliath boomed again. "Galen, do you think a reed can fell a tree? You are foolish! You are nothing and you never will be anything!"

Galen's shame deepened as the great warrior turned to Leander. "Galen fights like an Israelite. Isn't that right?"

Emboldened, Leander exclaimed, "Yes! He

punches the air as if it had breath, stabbing every-where but the target!"

Goliath threw back his huge head and laughed deep in his throat. "Very good, Leander!" The giant gently placed a massive hand on Leander's shoulder before adding, "Come to my tent and help me pre-pare to again insult those Israelite dogs yapping across the valley! Maybe this evening one of them will finally have the courage to accept my challenge."

Galen closed his eyelids tightly to stop the tears that threatened to slide out. He stood there in mis-ery, hearing the soldiers and Leander's followers drifting away while hurling scornful remarks over their shoulders.

Galen heard the ground crunch under a sandal next to him. He cautiously opened his eyes to see one of his friends anxiously looking at him.

"You all right?" Ziklag asked, lightly touching Galen's wrist where angry red welts were rising from Leander's hard blow.

Not sure he could trust himself to speak without his voice quivering, Galen only nodded. He was tempted to wipe away the fugitive tear that cruised unbidden down his right cheek, but he pretended it didn't exist.

"You could have beaten him," Ziklag declared with stout friendship. "He's two years older, taller, and outweighs you by thirty pounds, but you're brave and smart and quick. You had him down, fair and square, but he didn't fight fair. Otherwise, you would have won."

Galen found his voice. He bitterly exclaimed, "Goliath doesn't think so!"

"He missed seeing you take Leander down. Goliath only stepped from between the tents just before Leander tripped you."

Galen shrugged. "It doesn't make any difference, Zik. Goliath thinks I'm only a tiny ant, or a reed growing by the water." Galen's voice began to rise in anger. "But he's wrong! I'm a good fighter and am not afraid! I have a good head for thinking! I'll grow stronger, and I'll become a good warrior! You'll see!"

Zik protested, "You don't have to convince me! You're really strong for your age. More than that, I know from what you've been through that you're strong inside where it really counts. Next time, you'll beat Leander."

"I thought I had him today, but I was wrong," Galen sadly admitted. He bent and retrieved his shield but ignored the fallen branch. "Somehow," he mused, hefting the small round shield, "I've got to trade this in for the right to carry Goliath's shield."

Zik's eyes opened wide. "His shield? Have you ever tried to lift it?"

"No, but I can."

"I'm not so sure," Ziklag said uncertainly. "One time when Goliath was eating and drinking with the other soldiers, I slipped into his tent and picked up his bronze spear. The iron head alone must weigh between 15 and 25 pounds, so think how much heavier his shield has to be!"

"I don't care!" Galen said stubbornly. "Everything important in the world has been taken from me: my parents, my brother, my home. But when I carry Goliath's shield ahead of him into battle, all of our soldiers and even the Israelites will know I am somebody!"

"I hope you're right, Galen," his friend said sincerely. "But how are you going to do that?"

Pondering that question, Galen silently looked across the Valley of Elah where soon the Israelite army would gather, as they did every morning and evening. They had done this for more than a month while Goliath shouted insults and vainly called for the Israelites to send out one warrior to fight him, man-to-man.

But the inadequately armed Israelites had refused, knowing that if they sent a champion who lost to Goliath, all the others would become Philistine slaves.

Zik broke into Galen's musings to repeat his question. "So how are you going to do that?"

Galen firmly declared, "I don't know, but somehow I'll find a way. I must!"

CHAPTER 2

All through the heat of the desert afternoon, Galen and Ziklag sat in the shelter of the Philistine tents and stared thoughtfully across the Valley of Elah. The boys had exhausted all ideas of how to change Goliath's mocking insults into such admiration for Galen that he would be allowed to carry the giant's shield. In the cool of the evening, when both armies had gathered on their hillsides facing each other, Goliath would again shout his taunts across to the Israelites.

Zik changed his position as the sun eroded his shady spot. Lowering his voice, he said, "I don't blame the Israelites for not accepting Goliath's challenge. The Israelites only have wooden weapons while our people control the manufacture and use of iron and bronze. So we're not only the best warriors anywhere, but we're equipped with the finest weapons in the world."

Galen absently nodded, his eyes sweeping the small valley with its famous terebinth trees and seasonal wild flowers. A shimmering silver string along the valley floor marked a small stream. Galen shifted his gaze to the right where the Israelite camp showed movement.

Galen mused, "I think they're getting ready to eat. When they finish, they'll come out and form up as they always do when they know Goliath is about to make his usual challenge."

"Then we'd better go to my tent," Ziklag replied, standing up. "You know how my mother likes to have us show up on time when she's ready to serve the meal."

A heavy sigh escaped Galen as memory of his own late mother flooded his aching heart. He was grateful that Zik's family had taken him in and been kind to him. Still, nothing would ease the pain of having lost his entire family when disease carried them away. Galen still sometimes felt guilty because he alone had recovered.

As the evening cooled, Galen and Ziklag approached Goliath's tent where his armor-bearer had laid out the giant's usual coat of mail, helmet, greaves, spear, and javelin. The armor-bearer's job was to follow after Goliath and finish off anyone he cut down. Leander looked up from where he was carefully oiling Goliath's huge shield.

From his great height, Goliath looked down at Galen and Zik and laughed. "So, the ant dares show up in spite of the inglorious spectacle he made of himself earlier today!"

Galen pretended he didn't hear the mocking tone, or see the smirk on Leander's face. "I came," Galen began, taking a quick breath, "to ask to be your shield bearer for this evening."

Galen heard a surprised snort of derision from Leander, but Goliath narrowed his eyes and thoughtfully regarded Galen for a few seconds before answering. Then he shrugged his mighty shoulders. "Why not?"

Leander made a startled, choking sound. Goliath half-turned toward him and winked. Galen knew he wasn't supposed to have seen that, but it didn't matter. He had something to prove to both Goliath and

Leander, and it was only natural they would regard him with contempt.

The giant turned back to Galen and raised a huge arm that rippled with immense muscles. "Yes, why not?" he repeated. "Those fools across the valley will not fight. They will continue to cower like women."

Behind him, Zik whispered so softly that only Galen could hear, "He's saying that to mock you again."

Galen acknowledged his friend's warning with the barest nod. Galen knew it was a sad victory for him because Goliath didn't think him worthy to go anywhere near a fight. Yet his determination made him risk even more ridicule.

"Thank you," he told the giant, but his eyes shifted to the great shield. It was metallic and circular shaped with leather-wrapped wooden handles inside to hold it. For a fleeting moment, fear surged through Galen and instantly dried his mouth like the desert sand.

Goliath motioned with a hand as large as Galen's head. "Pick it up," the giant rumbled.

Unconsciously licking his lips, Galen nodded and crouched beside the shield. He heard suppressed laughter from Leander, but Galen concentrated on the job before him. Flexing his fingers, he slid his right arm through the leather straps. His eyes confirmed what he had been told. Shields were commonly made over a wood or wicker frame and covered with oiled leather. Goliath's circular shield was of wood and polished leather covered with bronze and reinforced with metal at the edges, making it very heavy.

Galen lifted one end so that he could better grasp a wooden and leather handle designed to give greater control. Even that small effort alarmed Galen because he realized that the shield weighed more than he had expected. He hesitated, fighting his concern.

With a curse, Goliath rumbled, "Go on! Pick it up!"

Galen braced his legs and back to provide maximum power. He had better control with the leather-wrapped wooden handle, so he closed his fingers firmly and jerked hard.

He was astonished at how the massive weight threatened to throw him off balance while he struggled to lift the edge of the shield from the floor.

Leander exclaimed with obvious delight in his

tone, "All the way! Lift it all the way off the floor!"

Straining every muscle and with great determination, Galen desperately tried to tilt the shield on edge to support it before setting it fully upright. It was useless. The dead weight threw him off balance.

He released his grip on the handle, but it was too late. The shield thudded back onto the ground and Galen fell ingloriously on top of it.

Goliath laughed so hard that Galen felt the shield vibrate beneath him. The giant taunted, "Galen, why don't you go join the women?"

"Yes!" Leander added through his laughter. "Join the women because you'll never be man enough to become a warrior!"

His face flaming with embarrassment, Galen blindly staggered out of the tent with Zik following. Mocking laughter chased after them.

By the time Goliath and his shield bearer, followed by his armor-bearer, walked out in front of the assembled Philistine soldiers to issue his nightly challenge to the Israelites, Galen believed everyone had heard of his humiliation with the shield.

He chose to sit at the back edge of the crowd

where he hoped to have some degree of freedom from the scornful laughter and jeering insults. He would have preferred to be alone in his misery, but Zik joined him in silent support.

Goliath, resplendent in his full armor and helmet, grandly strode out in front of the assembled Philistines. He cupped his huge hands around his mouth and shouted across to the opposite hillside where the Israelites were gathered, as usual.

"Why do you come out and line up for battle?" Goliath's words echoed across the valley and faded away.

He took a deep breath and called out again in his great booming voice, "Am I not a Philistine, and are you not the servants of Saul? Choose a man and have him come down to me. If he is able to fight and kill me, we will become your subjects; but if I kill him, then you will become our subjects and serve us."

Zik whispered, "I've heard him say that so many times, but it still stirs my blood to hear it again. Listen. Now he's going to say something more."

Goliath shouted across the valley. "This day I defy the ranks of Israel! Give me a man and let us fight each other!"

Again, the giant's words echoed across the valley and faded into silence. There was no answer from the Israelites. The stillness became so strong that Galen thought he could hear his own blood pounding against his eardrums. He was still sick at heart because of his inability to lift Goliath's shield.

I've got to show Goliath I am going to be a man and a great warrior! Galen thought in despair. *But how can I prove that to him?*

The answer came as silently as a thought, but with the power of a blow from Goliath's great arm. Galen suddenly reached out and clutched Zik's arm. "Come on! I know what I can do!"

CHAPTER 3

Galen hurriedly led Ziklag away behind the Philistine tents while everyone in camp still focused attention on the Israelites across the valley.

Zik complained, "Are you going to walk all the way to the Great Sea before you tell me your idea?"

"I want to make sure nobody hears us," Galen replied over his shoulder.

Galen passed the final tent and stopped, his eyes bright with excitement. "Zik, I know how to make Goliath change his mind about me!"

"Oh? How?"

Dropping his voice, Galen explained, "I'll sneak over to the Israelite camp and spy on them! I'll come back and report to Goliath how many men they have—"

"No!" Zik interrupted, throwing up his skinny

arms in protest. "They'll catch you and you'll get killed!"

Galen exclaimed, "No, they won't! I'll be very careful. I'll wait until after dark—"

"I still say no!" Zik broke in again, his thin voice rising in concern. "It's too dangerous!"

A voice from behind the tent asked, "What is?"

"Oh, no!" Galen muttered under his breath as a stout boy of about 12 stepped into sight followed by four other boys. "It's Gath and the other Philistine lords! They must have seen us slip away and followed us."

Zik didn't reply because the other boys were close enough to overhear. They swaggered proudly, pretending they were the young lords of the five main Philistine towns of Gaza, Ekron, Ashdod, Ashkelon, and Gath. From these communities, five adult male lords now ruled all Philistines. Each of the five boys had chosen to drop his given name to be known among friends by a town name. Gath had chosen his because Goliath came from there.

"What's too dangerous?" Gath repeated, stopping and bracing his legs belligerently in front of Galen and Zik. Two young Philistine lords flanked Gath on both sides and imitated his stance. Gath was the oldest in the group and a close friend of Leander.

Zik whispered, "Tell him, or they'll beat us up!"

The five young lords overheard and grinned without humor. Their hands simultaneously curled into hard fists.

Galen knew that Zik spoke the truth, but his insides lurched at the thought of sharing his grand plan with Gath and the others. Galen sadly recalled other times when the lords had either laughed at one of his ideas or stolen it.

Gath would also tell Leander, and that made Galen's stomach twist painfully. He imagined those boys going on the spying mission by themselves, leaving Galen behind.

Ashdod, the heaviest of the young lords, broke into Galen's thoughts. "Maybe you need us to give you a couple of good punches to make you talk!"

Gaza and Ekron sneered and started to say something, but Gath cut them off. "I'll handle this," he snapped.

The four lords fell silent.

Gulping, Galen thought of a risky possibility. "All right, but on one condition. It's my idea. If you don't like it, you must promise not to tell anyone until it's over. And if you do like it, then you must all promise that none of you will claim it was your idea."

Galen started to add, "And I'll be the leader," but decided against it. *Maybe*, he told himself, *they'll be afraid and not want to go into the enemy camp.*

Gath sneered, "We don't have to promise anything."

Galen shrugged. "Fine with me. Come on, Zik; let's go work out the details."

Zik's eyes widened in surprise as Galen turned and started away. Then, apparently realizing that the five bigger boys would force him to tell if he stayed, he called, "Wait, Galen! I'm coming!"

Galen stopped and waited until Zik reached him. As they walked off together, Galen heard the Philistine lords hurriedly whispering to each other.

Under his breath, Galen whispered to Zik, "That's a bad sign! I don't want them to know anything about this, but I'm afraid—"

Gath interrupted with a resigned expression. "You win, Galen! We all promise!"

Galen groaned in disappointment as the other lords nodded in agreement. Now he had to reveal his plan or else the five boys would spread word all over the camp that he and Zik were up to something.

"All right," Galen replied. "Gather around close so nobody hears, and I'll tell you."

———

Right away, Galen was sorry he had disclosed his plan. The five would-be lords whooped with joy at the idea and insisted on going along with Galen to spy on the Israelites. He protested vigorously, pointing out that one person had a better chance of succeeding in the mission than a small group. An argument erupted, so Gath declared they would ask Goliath's opinion.

Galen's mind was in turmoil. What if Goliath didn't like the idea? Or if he did, what if he approved of Gath's suggestion that all the boys go? Galen had planned to tell no one except Zik, and then to venture alone into the enemy camp. Galen's dreams of impressing the giant were starting to shred by the time the seven boys approached Goliath and his Philistine warriors.

They, with Leander on the edge of the group, sat on the hillside, laughing and talking. Shadows had filled in the Valley of Elah. On the opposite hill, the black goat-hair tents of the Israelites were barely visible in the light from their campfires.

Goliath had taken off his armor. Leander silently polished the giant's helmet as Gath jerked his thumb toward Galen. Before he could speak, Gath said, "He has a plan we thought you might like to hear about."

Galen resented Gath's use of "we," but he had to be content that Gath had kept his word and given credit for the idea to Galen. He briefly explained while the camp firelight chased shadows across Goliath's broad face.

When Galen finished, the other boys and all the warriors silently waited for cues from Goliath on how to react to the proposal.

"So," the giant's voice reverberated from his massive chest, "the little ant wants to be a flat-tailed scorpion and sting the Israelites in the night!"

Seeing a chance to salvage his original idea, Galen hastily added, "I'll go alone, so nobody else will be in danger."

"No!" Gath exclaimed. "We all go, even little Zik!"

A chorus of agreement came from all the other boys except Zik. He remained silent.

Leander dropped one of the giant's greaves. "Me, too!" he exclaimed. "I want to go!"

Galen's heart seemed to leap with disappointment and anger. Desperately he explained to Goliath, "This plan will work best if there's only me—"

The giant interrupted. "You want to be a warrior worthy of carrying my shield," he said thoughtfully. "No one gets to be a warrior by hiding in tents. You may not have done well this afternoon with my shield, Galen, but here's your chance to grow up a little. Go, spy out the enemy!"

Galen's misgivings vanished. "Thank you!" he cried, imagining the praise from Goliath the next morning when he heard the good report that Galen would bring him. "I'll make you proud," he added heartily.

"Maybe," Goliath agreed, "but after your failure this afternoon, I think you'd better have company. So, all of these boys will go with you except Leander!"

"But—!" Galen's disappointed protestation was lost in the roar of approval from all except Leander and Zik.

There was only a sliver of moon by the time the boys had each packed their small images of Dagon, the chief Philistine god. These wood carvings of a figure with a man's head, face, and upper body had a fish for the lower torso, and fins instead of feet. Dagon was supposed to protect the boys as they crossed the Valley of Elah.

Gath tried to take the lead, but Galen hurried ahead of him and stubbornly set a fast pace to keep his place. His heart thumped hard against his chest, but he wasn't sure if it was from the fast but silent walking, or fear. At first, Galen hadn't been frightened, especially when all the others were bragging about what they would do to the Israelites if they were older. But as they neared the enemy, fear crept into Galen's mind.

The stillness of the night and the deep shadows of trees and brush on the hillside where the enemy camped caused Galen some doubts. Twice he turned and hissed warnings to the young lords about making too much noise. They walked carefully, making a wide arc before coming up on the back side of the enemy's hillside camp. There Galen stopped in the dark shelter of some trees.

While the others caught their breath, Galen

whispered final instructions. "Remember what each of you is to do. Be very, very quiet. All our lives, we've been trained in warrior skills, so use them well. Count the tents in your section and try to see how many men sleep in each. Keep an eye out for any good weapons in sight, watch out for sentries, don't get seen or caught, then meet back here as fast as you can."

Zik asked with a slight tremor in his voice, "What if any of us do get taken prisoner?"

Before Galen could reply, Gath spoke. "You heard what Goliath and the other warriors said. We're on our own. If anything goes wrong, they'll claim that they didn't know anything about this trip. That way, nobody gets blamed but us. But I intend to succeed!"

Galen reached out in the darkness and laid a comforting hand on Zik's skinny arm. "Don't think about what Goliath said. Nobody's going to get caught."

Zik protested, "But what if we're seen?"

Gath made a disgusted sound in the night. "Where were you when that was discussed a while ago? We all run, scatter; take care of yourself as best you can."

Zik protested, "But you're all bigger and can run faster than I can!"

Gath laughed mockingly in the darkness. "Zik, you're afraid of everything! So maybe you should go back before you get us all in trouble."

"I make the decisions here!" Galen said sternly, refusing to release his role as leader and the honor Goliath would give him when the mission was a success. "We all go forward."

"Uh," one of the young Philistine lords said hesitantly, "I could take Zik back if he's scared."

Galen recognized Ekron's voice. He sounded as if he was frightened but was trying to hide his fear by offering to do a good thing.

"We all stay," Galen said softly but firmly. "Zik, I could use an extra pair of eyes with me. Come help me out. Everyone else, spread out and be careful!"

Galen heard a disgusted snort from Gath, who no doubt resented taking orders from Galen. But Gath didn't say anything as everyone silently moved off in preassigned directions.

In moments, again moving as quietly as possible, Galen and Zik stealthily approached the back of the first row of Israelite tents. These were faintly visible from the glow of the campfires, which had burned low.

Galen wasn't afraid because he was so determined to be a hero. That would have been easier if only he had been there alone. Now he would have to share the glory with the other boys.

Unless, he thought, *I can do something so special that it'll stand out far above what Gath or any of the others do.*

He felt the reassuring weight of Dagon in his tunic as he stealthily crouched low, rounded the first tent, and peered inside. Two men snored loudly.

Easing away from that tent, he glanced around to see that Zik was doing the same with the tent in the opposite row. Gliding on away from his friend, silent as a serpent, Galen heard only his racing blood thumping against his eardrums and the snoring of Israelite men.

Galen tried to think of something spectacular he could do to impress Goliath. *Maybe I can get inside a tent and take a spear from beside an Israelite!*

Barely breathing from excitement, with blood now scalding through his body, Galen paused in the shadows of the nearest tent and furtively surveyed the whole camp.

There was no sign of the other boys, no unusual sound to give them away. Galen thought he glimpsed a shadowy figure dart from between some tents three rows over. A campfire there flared up briefly as the figure moved; Galen wasn't sure he had actually seen anyone.

He turned his attention back to the next tent in line. He was now deep inside the camp and far away from the trees and safety.

He noted the number of sleeping warriors and the types of weapons within easy reach of each man: poorly made bows, arrows, and crude spears. Cautiously, fearful the Israelite would awaken and catch him at his side, Galen bent and gently felt the spear point.

Just as I thought, he told himself with satisfaction. *It's all wood—even the point. It's been hardened in the fire, but it's still very inferior to our Philistine ones of iron or bron—*

His thoughts snapped off as the sleeping man stopped snoring and rolled over toward Galen. He froze, holding his breath. His heart tried to beat a hole in his chest.

After agonizing seconds, the soldier began snoring again. Galen still held his breath until he slipped outside the tent, his mouth dry as the desert sand.

That was close! he thought, glancing around. *I didn't dare risk taking his spear or drinking water. I still need something like that, but not from just any tent! Maybe their leader's! What's his name? Saul? Yes, King Saul! His tent must be marked in some special way.*

Galen crouched down and probed the rows of tents with eager eyes. For safety reasons, the leader often pitched his tent in the middle of the others.

There! By the dying light of a campfire, Galen glimpsed a pennant flying from a staff in front of a tent three rows away. *That must be his! Now if I can just take something from beside his head.*

Interrupting himself, Galen took a careful step, then again froze as someone moved outside the next tent. With wildly racing heart, Galen waited until the other person passed a campfire. *It's Gath!*

Without realizing it, Galen had sucked in his breath when he glimpsed the other boy. In thoughtless relief, he exhaled in a soft rush.

The sound made Gath spin around and leap back. He fell over the dying campfire and involuntarily cried out. He leaped up, frantically beating at flames licking at his clothes while Israelites in the adjacent tents jumped up, shouting in alarm.

"Philistines! They're everywhere! Get them!"

Israelites poured out of their tents, weapons in hand, while the alarm cry of "Philistines!" echoed from other areas of the camp.

Trailing smoke but no fire, Gath darted wildly through the tents, racing for his life toward the valley.

Galen knew the other boys were also running, but he fought the temptation. He was farthest from the valley, so he forced himself to stand between the tents while all their occupants chased the fugitives. Galen, frozen with fright, was unnoticed in the darkness.

He recognized Zik's voice shouting, "Wait for me!"

Galen knew his friend was vainly trying to catch up with the older boys, but they wouldn't wait for him.

In moments, the entire camp had been emptied as the men pursued shadowy fugitives off the hillside and into the valley now wrapped in the black of night. All alone, Galen's heart hammered in fear. Gooseflesh rippled down his arms, and his mouth instantly went dry. Trying to control his fright, he started to turn and head uphill into the trees. He planned to circle wide, enter the valley some distance away, and return to his own camp.

Then he stopped and looked back. The king's flag was still visible in the glow of the campfire.

Galen took a quick breath and sprinted to the tent. He didn't even break stride as he snatched the staff from the ground. He rounded the tent and raced between the rows, triumphantly heading back for the trees with the trophy in his hand!

CHAPTER 4

For two hours, Galen crouched in the trees behind the Israelites' camp, clutching his prize. Galen felt confident that Goliath would be impressed when he saw the king's flag. But it was too risky to move because the Hebrew soldiers were as agitated as bees in a disturbed beehive.

Galen cautiously peered over the top of a log as fuel was added to the campfires. In the bright blaze of the fires, he could see the Israelite warriors spread out, diligently searching for the night invaders. Galen's rapidly beating heart and ragged breathing settled down only when the troops finally drifted back to the fires.

Galen saw that none of his friends was among them. The Israelites didn't return to their tents, but stood around talking angrily. Their tones confirmed that they had failed to catch anyone, not even Zik.

Even if only one boy had been captured, there would have been celebrating.

When the excitement and campfires died down, full darkness slowly returned. Then, knowing he had to start his dash for safety across the Valley of Elah's open, nearly treeless plain before daylight, Galen clutched his pennant, bent nearly double, and circled away from the camp. When he thought it was safe, he cut back toward the valley. Breathing hard, and still crouched low, he paused at the edge of the plain. He looked around one last time before starting his run.

That's when he saw the sentry coming toward him.

If Galen hadn't been bent down, he would not have seen the dark silhouette of the Israelite against the faint light of the horizon. Silently laying down the banner, Galen dropped flat on his stomach. Gripping the banner, he crept under a bush by a little brook. The water made pleasant sounds as it passed over small stones. Galen hoped it covered the swishing sound of the disturbed bush and the semi-controlled noise of his labored breathing.

He had lost sight of the sentry, but could hear the sound of a spear being thrust experimentally into bushes as the sentry slowly moved toward him.

Stifling a groan, Galen lay perfectly still. He was terribly frightened, alone, and in mortal danger. Even if the sentry didn't find him, others must also be on guard in the night, watching and listening.

I have to get across the valley before daylight! he repeatedly reminded himself. He dared not try crossing when he could easily be seen. He could not outrun an arrow or spear—not even ones made of inferior wood.

Galen's ears followed the slow, deliberate approach of the Israelite sentry. In moments, he would be at the dense bush where Galen lay flat. His heart raced and his mouth was dry as only terror could make it.

He realized his breathing had increased so sharply that it made a rasping sound. He tried holding it as the sound of the sentry's footsteps stopped at his bush.

He flinched as the spear plunged into the foliage over his head. He flattened his body against the ground and pressed his face into the dirt, turning his head only enough to breathe.

Hold your breath! Galen sternly warned himself. *Don't move!* His skin crawled as he remembered the fire-hardened spear points he had seen in the Israel-ite camp. One of those fearsome weapons was now repeatedly thrust haphazardly into the high portion of the bush.

His imagination brought the spear point closer and closer toward him. Closer . . . closer.

He stoutly held back the tears that threatened to leak out from his tightly shut eyelids. After all, he was 10, and Philistine boys were taught from an early age to be warriors and bear up under all circumstances.

Besides, Galen intended to win Goliath's favor and be honored by carrying his shield. But in the black of night, cut off from his people, Galen was also a little boy with a deadly problem. Except for seizing the king's pennant, almost everything had gone wrong with Galen's plan to do a daring deed all by himself. And now, this.

He could only wait, hearing the sentry's spear sliding in and out of the bush inches from his body as the soldier tried to make sure no one was hiding there. It was all Galen could do to not leap up and make a wild dash for the valley as the spear point struck the ground between his right arm and chest.

as futile, so he stayed frozen as the spear
rawn.

led himself to not think about it. He tried
self by remembering that the other six
ped. Just when Galen could not hold
nger, the sentry moved on.

quietly as possible, he took another
held it until he was sure the sentry
away. Satisfied, Galen released the
tried to relax.

t, and gloom seeped into his mind
escaped this time, but if he moved
uld surely hear him. He had no
where he was for a while.

where the other sentries were and
his sentinel would walk before he
r now, Galen was safe, but what
hen dawn came?

o *something!* he sternly reminded
at? Stay here and risk being caught?
l into the valley and hope they don't
m out of bow shot?

ated, he shifted his cramped position
aching muscles. Beside him, he felt the
he pennant that he had snatched from

outside the Israelite king's tent. But v
would that do if Galen didn't return to tri
show it to everyone?

He reached into his tunic and gently
image of Dagon. Galen hoped to feel
as he fingered the carving of the hal

He had often heard his Philistin
this god. Dagon was the principal
in the two Philistine cities of G
Galen's father had come from
from Ashdod.

Mother, he thought, closing h
his forehead on his forearms wh
on the ground. His mind escaped
of the moment by retreating to c
ries. He could see her, hear her
touch . . .

He realized he was getting sleep
such comfort in the memories that
closed and sorted through recollec
holding him, her voice soft and tende
him. He had often gone to sleep in he
in her love.

Then death had taken her; taken h
followed by her husband and their othe

But that w
was withd

He wil
to cheer him
boys had escap
his breath any lo

Exhaling as
quick breath and
was still moving
pennant staff and

But he couldn'
and heart. He had
now, the sentry wo
choice but to wait

He wondered
how far away t
turned back. Fo
would happen w

I have to de
himself. *But wh*
Or try to craw
see me until I'

As he deb
to ease his
staff with t

vhat good

umphantly

touched the

some comfort

f-man, half-fish.

e family speak of

god worshipped

aza and Ashdod.

Gaza, his mother

his eyes and resting

ere he sprawled flat

the terrible reality

omforting memo-

voice, feel her

y, but there was

he kept his eyes

tions. She was

r as she sang to

r arms, secure

her suddenly,

son.

"No!" Galen whispered aloud, startling himself. He realized with a start that he had dozed, had dreamed.

Frightened again, he quickly but quietly pushed the foliage aside. There was no sign of the sentry. Galen strained to hear until he could hear the blood throbbing in his eardrums, but there was no sound of nearby sentries.

Relieved, he wearily dropped his head and tried to recall more memories about his mother when he was younger. She held him by the hand. She had done that the first time she had led him through the marketplace with its strange smells and sights and sounds. He had looked up apprehensively, but she smiled reassuringly. It was almost as good a feeling as being hugged closely . . .

I was dreaming again! The knowledge hit him hard as he lifted his head and blinked, then frowned. The sun probed slender, warm fingers through the bush where the spear had broken some limbs. *Daylight!* That realization struck him even harder. With trembling fingers, he pushed the leaves aside from his hiding place.

There was a great stillness; a silence so profound that it puzzled him while his eyes wildly skimmed the Israelite tents. There wasn't a soldier in sight. With sudden hope, Galen twisted to look at the small Valley of Elah. It was wide open, friendly, beckoning to him. He started to get to his feet, but his entire body was stiff from inactivity.

A frenzied desire to dash across the narrow valley toward his people seized him. But where were the Israelites? How close? He couldn't see them. He listened and heard faint voices from beyond a hill past the camp. Puzzled, he darted a look across the valley, and then he knew.

The Philistine warriors were slowly gathering on the side of the hill in preparation for Goliath's morning challenge. That meant the Israelites were also assembling just out of Galen's sight, beyond the hill, where they could see the giant when he appeared again.

Galen's hopes leaped like a wild stag, then crashed. He realized he could not cross the valley now. Both sides would see him. His people might try to come to his aid, but the Israelites were so close they would run him down or fill him with arrows and spears before he got far.

I've caused a lot of grief for everyone, he chided himself. *Now what should I do?*

He didn't know, but he was keenly aware that he was very thirsty. He checked to make sure that no Israelite soldier was around, then he crawled out of his hiding place and down to the brook. He cupped his hands together and gulped the fresh, cool water.

It felt so good that he closed his eyes and splashed another double handful of water on his face. It was so wonderful that he gave himself totally to the joy of repeating the process.

A footstep sounded behind him. His eyes popped open. A human towered over him.

Shocked, Galen started to scramble to his feet, horrified that he had been careless—something no aspiring Philistine warrior should do. But Galen knew it was too late to escape when a shadow fell across him.

He glanced up and glimpsed an Israelite standing just three feet away!

With a racing heart, Galen tried to crawl away, but was stopped by the bush where he had hidden all night. Trapped, he again glanced up and realized that the shadow was cast by an Israelite boy about his own age. He had dark eyes and hair, but didn't look too strong, although he carried empty water skins.

Galen told himself, *I can handle him!* He stood up but remained alert, glancing around to make sure no other Israelites were near.

"Hello," the strange boy said calmly, lowering the water skins from his shoulder. "Don't you have a brook on your side of the valley?"

"Um, well, uh, yes." Galen hurriedly looked around, fearful that some adult Israelite would see him. He was relieved that there was no one in sight except the boy.

The boy took an empty skin and plunged it into the stream before asking, "Then what are you doing here?"

Galen hesitated. He was a truthful boy, but it would be dangerous to tell all the facts. After all, this was an Israelite boy and an enemy of the Philistines. Galen tried to think how to tell the truth without revealing all of it. "Uh . . ." he finally replied, "some friends and I were out . . . uh . . . exploring. They, well, they ran off and left me."

His excuse sounded a little lame to his own ears, but he felt that he had been truthful enough.

The other boy lifted the filled water skin from the brook. He observed, "You're a long way from your people."

Galen bristled and went on the offensive. It seemed logical since the stranger showed no signs of aggression. Galen spread his feet and scowled, demanding firmly, "Are you saying I'm a liar?"

The other boy shrugged. "No. I was just commenting, that's all."

Satisfied that his aggressive attitude seemed to be working and wasn't arousing any resentment, Galen added, "Well, it's a good thing you didn't call me a liar!"

Again, the Israelite boy took no offense. He thrust the next skin under the water. It bubbled as the air in it was displaced. He said, "My name's Reuben."

Galen automatically answered, "I'm Galen."

Reuben grinned up at him. "I've heard the name a few times. It means 'healer' in Greek."

Galen replied, "I like my name."

Reuben nodded. "No doubt you were named for some of your Philistine ancestors who originated in the Greek Isles before settling on the coast of the Great Sea."

Surprised and annoyed that the boy knew this, Galen felt it was necessary to say something he figured Reuben wouldn't know about the Philistines. Proudly, he announced, "We're called the Sea People, and we're great warriors."

"I've heard that said," Reuben admitted. He lifted the filled skin from the brook before adding, "But you must have heard how my ancestors defeated all the kings of tribes that used to live in this land."

"Rumors!" Galen scoffed. "The only great warriors are us Philistines! You Israelites have inferior weapons, and your men are farmers pretending to be soldiers. But we Philistines have the finest weapons and the most organized and well-trained soldiers anywhere. Right now, they're gathering on the hillside across the valley, waiting for Goliath to challenge one of your warriors to come fight him." Throwing out his chest, Galen added, "Someday, I will carry Goliath's shield!"

Reuben didn't seem impressed, so Galen quickly continued, "No Israelite will face Goliath because if your people sent a challenger, he'd be defeated, and all the rest of you would become our slaves."

"My forefathers were slaves in Egypt a long time ago," Reuben replied, standing and drying his hands on his tunic. "We are free now, and this is all going to be our land." He slowly turned and swept his arms in a wide circle. "All of it," he added.

Galen bristled again. "You're wrong! You're saying the Israelites will defeat my people, yet not one man in your army will even answer Goliath's challenge, let alone fight him!"

"Our God fights for us," Reuben replied calmly.

"Your God?" Galen laughed shortly. "I've heard about him. He can't even be seen because he doesn't exist!" Galen reached under his cloak and brought out the small replica of his fish-man god and silently held it up.

Reuben asked, "What's that?"

Galen exclaimed in disbelief, "You don't know who Dagon is?"

Reuben laughed. "That's Dagon? That silly little thing is your god you think can help you?"

Offended, Galen cried, "And who helps you? You have only one god, and you can't even *see* him! What kind of god is that?"

Reuben opened his mouth to answer as Goliath's daily morning challenge echoed across the Valley of Elah.

Galen puffed with pride. "That's Goliath!" Pointing across the plain, he continued, "See him standing out there in front of our warriors? Twice a day he does that, and nobody from your side even answers him because your invisible God is no match for Dagon and Goliath!"

Reuben shrugged. "Our God will prove you're wrong."

Laughing, Galen challenged, "When? How?"

"I don't know, but it's not up to me to know such things," Reuben replied calmly. "But when it happens, I want to be there to see it, so I watch twice a day."

He placed the last water skin on the bank, turned around, and pointed. "I go up on that little hill where I can see everything. You want to come with me?"

Fearful of being seen, Galen shook his head.

"Too bad," Reuben said. "Everyone's gone to watch the soldiers, so nobody's around here to see you. But from up on the hill, we could see both my people's warriors and yours without anyone seeing us. Sure you don't want to come with me?"

Galen glanced longingly at the open plain but knew that his flight would take him within view of the Israelites. They would not let him cross. He would have to wait for a better opportunity.

"Well," he said, "maybe just for a minute."

———————

Galen followed Reuben up to a small rock outcropping on top of the hill. It had an opening wide enough for two boys to lie on their stomachs. Only their heads showed.

Galen's heart swelled with pride. Across the valley, Goliath stood like a mighty stone pillar in front of the assembled Philistine army. The morning sun reflected off the soldiers' iron and brass weapons. They looked invincible as Goliath cupped his hands and once again roared his challenge.

Dropping his gaze to the Israelite army on their side of the valley, Galen almost sneered. "They're nothing but sheep herders and farmers! They don't even look like soldiers! And their weapons—why, the branches my friends and I play with are better than what your soldiers have."

"Looks aren't what count," Reuben declared. "In fact, it wouldn't matter if your entire Philistine army was filled with Goliaths. All true might and true power come from God."

Galen laughed. "That's the most stupid thing I've ever heard!"

For the first time, Galen's barbed words caused Reuben to react angrily. "You take that back!"

"No! I said it and I meant it!"

"Look, Galen, I've taken your insults about my people, but I will not let you dishonor my God!"

For a moment, the boys glared at each other, then the fear and frustration that had engulfed Galen all night suddenly exploded. Yelling, he leaped upon Reuben.

CHAPTER 6

The boys scuffled on the hillside, panting and tumbling over each other while struggling to gain the upper hand. Galen was surprised at how strong Reuben was, but reminded himself that he was a Philistine and Reuben was only an Israelite, so naturally the Israelite had to lose.

Reuben obviously didn't know that, because he rapidly rolled aside when Galen tried to pin him on his back. Galen was startled to find Reuben suddenly sitting on his chest.

Looking down at Galen, Reuben puffed, "Had enough?"

"No!" With a mighty effort, Galen squirmed free and tried to leap to his feet. They flew out from under him. He fell on his back and started sliding downhill. He instinctively reached out to grab something to hold onto. His fingers clamped down hard on Reuben's ankle, pulling him down. The boys tumbled together down the hillside.

They were stopped at the bottom by rolling into a small shrub that slashed them with sharp thorns.

Yelping in pain, they hurriedly freed themselves while trying to catch their breath. Galen felt small wounds on his hands and face from the rough ride and the shrub's stickers. Reuben's right cheek was scratched and his tunic torn.

Galen managed to puff, "Now have you had enough?"

Reuben hesitated, then said, "I have if you have."

Galen pounced on that. He wasn't so sure now that he could triumph over the Israelite, but he didn't want to give Reuben that impression. "Well," Galen replied, still trying to catch his breath, "I guess I'll let you go."

Reuben surprised him by grinning. "I was going to say the same thing."

In spite of himself, Galen returned the grin before changing the subject. "Do you suppose any of your people answered Goliath's challenge?"

Reuben glanced back up the hill. "Let's go see."

The boys were too late. The giant's challenge had gone unanswered, and the humiliated Israelites were slowly returning to their camps with downcast eyes.

The stark reality of Galen's situation hit him hard. He still could not safely leave until nightfall, so he would have to return to his hiding place by the brook. He had not eaten since the night before, yet he dared not risk foraging in daylight. He certainly wasn't going to ask an enemy of his people to bring him something.

When Galen was again safely hidden, Reuben shouldered his filled water skins and departed. This left Galen with another concern. *What if he tells his people where I am?*

In spite of the shade under the bush, the morning sun soon made it uncomfortably hot. He tried to ignore his annoyance and minor pains by dozing off.

He slept fitfully, dreaming that his mother was preparing all kinds of good things to eat. That included his favorite: fresh bread and cheese. It really smelled wonderful, but when he reached for it, it vanished. He moaned in his sleep.

When he awoke the good fragrance still lingered in his nostrils. He sniffed, his stomach growling in hunger. The scent persisted. He lifted his head and looked in the direction from which it seemed to come. Through the foliage, he saw a cut of cheese and two small loaves under the outside branches.

Hardly daring to believe what he saw, he squirmed around under the bush and touched the food. It was real!

Reuben! he thought. He quickly pulled the cheese and loaves into his shelter. He gobbled the delicious meal, marveling at what his people's enemy had done for him.

———

It was the longest, most tension-filled day of Galen's life. From time to time, Israelite soldiers walked past his hiding place. Older boys, too young to fight but eager to be helpful, periodically hurried past on errands for the warriors. Once, Galen held his breath as a youth briefly paused by his bush to drink from the brook. But no one noticed Galen.

Still, it was a huge relief when the sun dipped low. Galen consoled himself with the thought that it would soon be dark and he could slip back to his own camp.

As Galen eagerly anticipated rejoining his own

people, Reuben returned with his water skins.

Stiff and sore from the long enforced inactivity and the cuts and bruises of the morning, Galen slid out from under his hiding place. He stood up but stayed close to the bush so others couldn't see him.

He felt awkward about expressing his gratitude to an enemy of his people, but he felt he must. "Those were really good loaves and cheese," he said.

Reuben lowered the water skins to the brook side. "Glad you liked them. Will your mother be worried because you didn't get back to your camp last night?"

Galen sadly lowered his head. "She's dead. So's my father and my brother. I'm living with—" His voice started to break, and he turned away to hide the unwelcome tears that suddenly misted his vision.

Reuben didn't say anything, but reached out and gave Galen a quick pat on the shoulder.

He sniffed loudly and turned back to face the other boy. "I don't care! What is a family, anyway? Warriors are tough and don't need families."

"Well, my family is mighty important to me," Reuben replied. "We're farmers, like many Hebrews. All Israel is really one big family, so I'm a part of that, too. But in my own family, I'm the oldest son, so father lets me help the soldiers, like filling the water skins twice a day."

Hesitating, Reuben added, "Would you like to hear a couple of stories about my family?"

Galen wasn't going anywhere until full nightfall, and he was lonely, so he nodded and listened. Galen's memory of his own brother suddenly overwhelmed him, and he turned away again.

Reuben surprised him by saying, "I think you really do care about your family."

Fighting to maintain control, Galen suddenly jumped up. "Let's have a play-fight!" He wasn't sure that was a safe thing to do, but he'd said it, so he glanced around and was relieved to see that nobody was in sight. He spotted a couple of dry branches that had fallen off a nearby tree. "Here," he said, "let's use these."

The boys grabbed them and stripped off all small twigs, leaving only four-foot-long sticks. They began flailing at each other, but not hard. No matter how Galen tried to thrust, Reuben parried. They fought for several minutes with the sticks banging together, but not a single blow landed on either person.

"I'm wearing you down!" Galen cried, trying to

convince with words what he was not doing with force.

"You're wrong!" Reuben replied, just as Goliath's challenge echoed across the valley. Instantly stepping back out of Galen's reach, Reuben said, "Listen!"

Galen was glad for an excuse to stop the mock battle. He strained to hear, then nodded.

"Good!" Reuben exclaimed. "Nobody will see you because they've all gone to see Goliath, so let's go watch!"

"That's fine with me, but I won," Galen replied proudly. He believed that and felt very good about it. However, he was disappointed to see that Reuben wasn't even distressed as he casually turned toward the hill.

Galen dropped his stick and followed, puzzled. Winning was important to him, even in play, but it didn't seem to trouble Reuben.

———

From their hiding place in the rock cleft at the top of the hill, Galen gazed down on the backs of the silent Israelite soldiers. He could tell from the slump of their shoulders and the way they kept looking down that they were discouraged as Goliath again called his challenge.

Without looking at Reuben, Galen asked, "How can your people stand there like sheep while Goliath insults them day after day?"

"Like our leader, King Saul, they are all waiting."

Reuben's calm, assured reply made Galen turn toward him. "Waiting for what?"

"For God to send someone to defeat Goliath."

Galen laughed loudly. "A puny Israelite defeat Goliath? That's not possible. Why, I've seen him in many battles, and he's always won."

When Reuben didn't answer, Galen added proudly, "And someday I will also be a great Philistine warrior! I will be as feared and as well-known as Goliath!"

Reuben smiled but did not mock Galen. "You may be a great warrior, but before then, God will defeat Goliath in His own way."

The confident words troubled Galen, but he couldn't be sure why. He blustered, "We'll see about that! Why, there isn't a man alive—"

Reuben suddenly gripped his arm and hissed, "Don't move! A soldier's coming this way!"

CHAPTER 7

Both boys froze; only their eyes followed the Israelite sentry patrolling along the brook side at the base of the hill where the boys hid. Suddenly, the soldier stopped and bent over.

"He's found my water skins!" Reuben whispered. "He will probably start looking around to see who left them."

Without waiting for Galen's response, Reuben stood up. "You stay here and don't move until I get him to leave! I hope you make it safely back to your camp tonight!"

Galen stayed dead still as he watched the Israelite boy approach the sentry, then bend down and casually fill the water skins. They talked until the skins were full, then walked off together. Galen wondered if he would have done the same for Reuben.

Three hours passed slowly before it was totally dark and the Israelites' campfires had burned low. Sentries were some distance away. Galen gripped the banner he had taken from the Israelite commander's tent the night before. Galen hoped he was right about it having been King Saul's. He decided he would tell Goliath that it certainly was Saul's. This news would surely make the giant treat him with respect.

Preparing to return to his camp, Galen silently slid out from under the bush where he had spent the day. He wrapped the banner around the staff and held it in his left hand. He crawled on hands and knees into the Valley of Elah until he was out of bow shot. Then he stood up and ran hard through the night.

He could just imagine the astonished looks on his friends' faces when he showed them the prize. But he was most eager to impress Goliath. *He'll never forget what a brave thing I did*, Galen assured himself. *When I'm older and stronger, he'll let me carry his shield because of this deed!*

As Galen neared his camp, a Philistine sentry challenged him. Galen identified himself and was promptly escorted to the officer in charge of sentries.

Galen was disappointed because he had expected to be taken directly to Goliath, but the officer started asking questions. "How did you escape? All those boys with you claimed you were captured."

Galen repeated what had happened to him, and proudly unwrapped the flag from around the staff. "I took it from inside King Saul's tent," Galen declared, waving the banner and feeling his little addition to the facts wasn't really lying.

He added, "He never heard or saw me," then immediately felt guilty even though this was true because Saul had already left the tent.

The officer was more interested in knowing about the Israelites than about how the boy got the flag. He asked Galen, "How many warriors do they have? How well equipped are they? What weapons do they carry? Do they have anything except wooden spears and javelins?"

Galen answered as best he could, but omitted any mention of Reuben. As he spoke, he vainly hoped that Goliath would arrive to hear his story. However, when the officer finally dismissed Galen, he stepped outside the tent and was greeted by most of the small male civilian population and walking wounded soldiers who had heard about his return.

He was pleased to see Ziklag and the other boys who'd gone on the raid with him, but they were forced to stay in the background while the men bombarded him with more questions.

They heartily congratulated him on his escape and begged to hear details of his adventure. He obliged, almost strutting with pride. He showed his captured pennant and declared that he had snatched it from inside King Saul's own tent. The exclamations at this news encouraged Galen to tell them about hiding under the bush until it was safe to return. Again, he chose to not mention Reuben.

Unlike his mostly factual account of his experience as he had described it to the officers, Galen embellished this version. He made it sound much more exciting and dangerous than it had really been. This brought loud exclamations of admiration from his audience.

Finally the older people allowed the younger ones to take their turn asking questions. By the light of the built-up campfires, Galen saw that the five young lords who had fled from the enemy camp now regarded him with open envy. However, Zik's eyes were different. Galen saw signs of tears in them.

Zik exclaimed in a trembling tone, "I thought you were dead!"

Galen lightly punched Zik on his shoulder. "I can take care of myself!"

Zik asked, "Weren't you scared?"

"Not even for a moment!" The second he said it, Galen felt another twinge of guilt. *I shouldn't have lied to Zik*, he told himself.

A young soldier pushed through the ring of admirers. "Galen," he announced, "Goliath sent me to say he wants to see you first thing tomorrow morning."

Galen was so proud that he felt he could almost float. He whispered to Zik, "Maybe Goliath wants to tell me that I can start training to be his shield bearer."

"Could be," Zik replied before adding, "We'd better get some sleep so you'll be at your best before him tomorrow."

Galen was reluctant to leave his admirers, but he nodded and followed his friend to the family tent.

———

The sun had not yet risen when Galen took the captured Israelite banner and appeared with it at the giant's tent. Goliath's tent was much higher, longer, and wider than any other tent in camp. A young soldier stationed outside said Goliath was expecting him.

Galen stepped in, expecting well-deserved praise and perhaps the coveted offer to someday be the giant's shield bearer. However, one look at Goliath made Galen feel unsure.

Even sitting down and without his armor, the Philistines' champion looked huge. He had no neck, Galen decided. The great head seemed to rest on massive shoulders above biceps that rippled with powerful muscles. He did not speak, but belched crudely and fixed Galen with bloodshot eyes.

That surprised Galen who had expected at least a look of appreciation. He asked, "You sent for me?"

Slowly, the giant stood up, towering impressively above the boy whom he regarded with cold, hard eyes. "Where were you yesterday?" the giant rumbled.

Galen blinked in surprise and tipped his head far back to look up at the famous warrior. "I was in the Israelite camp," he explained, then added hurriedly, "I thought you must have heard—"

"I heard," Goliath interrupted. He seemed bored as he scratched himself and asked, "Did you kill anyone?"

Galen was shocked. He was only 10 and had been on an adventure filled with danger and excitement, but he hadn't thought of killing anyone. Realizing that he was not about to receive the praise he expected, Galen answered in a low, quiet voice. "Uh . . . no. I didn't."

Goliath's lip curled in a sneer. "You were in the enemy's camp all that time, and you didn't kill a single person? What did you do—hide like an old woman?"

Galen licked suddenly dry lips, unsure what to say.

The giant's deep voice reverberated from his massive chest when he spoke again. "You want to someday carry my shield and become a Philistine soldier, but you don't seem to know what a real soldier does."

Towering over the boy, Goliath declared, "Soldiers kill; that's their purpose in war. Those Israelite dogs are our enemies! You must have had a chance to strike at least one, so why didn't you?"

Trembling with sudden alarm, Galen gulped,

thought of Reuben, and stuttered, "I . . . I . . . well . . ."

The giant interrupted in a voice that boomed like distant thunder. "The very least you could have done is to have harmed someone! That would have made you a man; and much more so if you had struck down some Israelite and brought back his possessions—at least a sword or spear."

Galen tried not to tremble at the giant's growing rage. Goliath scoffed, "Instead, Galen, you brought us a stick with a rag on it." He motioned toward Galen's trophy and added, "I doubt your story. I don't think you really risked your life for this. My guess is that you waited until all the Israelites were out of camp and you were alone when you picked it up."

Galen cringed at the scornful words. He found himself having trouble breathing. He thought of saying he was sorry, but decided to remain mute while Goliath glared at him.

Finally the giant asked harshly, "You really want to someday carry my shield and become a Philistine warrior?"

Suddenly hopeful again, Galen exclaimed, "Oh, yes!"

"Good!" the giant clapped an enormous hand on the boy's shoulder. "The only way to ever do that is to return to the enemy camp and at least hurt someone, if not kill him. So do it tonight, and bring proof! Do you understand?"

Galen reeled backward at the idea. He wanted to protest, but knew he must not. Slowly, sick at heart, he managed to mumble, "Yes, I understand."

The giant's heavy hand lifted from Galen's shoulder and came down with a resounding smack on his backside. "Good! Tell the sentry outside my tent to give you a stout club to take with you. Until you return with proof that you've earned the right to be a Philistine soldier, stay out of my sight!"

———————

All the joy and excitement of Galen's Israelite adventure had drained out of him at the giant's terrible assignment. Galen was too ashamed to even confide his problem to Zik. All day, he avoided other people and walked alone on the hillside overlooking the Valley of Elah. In his pain and anger, Galen desperately ached for the comfort always given him by his parents when he hurt. But they were long cold in their graves. Then Galen vainly caressed Dagon, his fish-man god, and sought guidance from it. But it felt cold and lifeless; a piece of wood carved by someone's hands. He wondered how Reuben called on his invisible God when he needed Him, and if He answered better than Dagon.

As the sun eased toward the western horizon, Galen heard some older boys playing at being warriors. At first, he ignored them, then he realized they were watching him and whispering. They knew what Goliath had required Galen to do. Everyone in camp must know now. The only good thing was that Galen realized the boys were pretending to be him, and he was brave.

They repeatedly acted out his striking down an Israelite so he could be a Philistine warrior and carry Goliath's shield. The boys carried on their mock battles until Goliath's evening challenge sent them running to see if an Israelite dog would dare meet the giant in one-on-one combat. Galen didn't move, but stayed alone in anguish.

Before the stars sprinkled the darkness with tiny points of light, Galen had reduced his choices to the absolute basics. He could either stay in camp and be disgraced and treated with contempt, or he could return to the Israelite camp and carry out Goliath's order.

Galen knew he might be killed, but wasn't it worth the risk if he succeeded and became a Philistine warrior worthy of carrying the great Goliath's shield?

With a heavy sigh, Galen made his choice. He picked up the heavy club given him by Goliath's sentry and made sure that his Dagon image was in his tunic. Setting his jaw in firm determination, Galen slipped unseen away from the Philistine encampment and headed across the valley toward the Israelite camp.

He would watch for a lone Israelite, then strike quickly and hard before losing his nerve. Then he would grab up whatever possessions the Israelite had and vanish into the night.

It was a terrible thing for a 10-year-old boy to do, but Galen reminded himself that he was a Philistine, taught from early childhood to be a mighty warrior. He mentally prepared himself for what he must do.

Using the faint light of the Israelite campfires, Galen found his way across the valley and back to the brook with the bush where he had previously hidden out. He barely heard the brook's murmur when his heart leaped at the sight of a lone figure standing there. The firelight was too faint to show his features, but that didn't matter. *It's probably better that way*, Galen thought.

Taking a deep breath and holding the club low so it wouldn't be seen, Galen quietly got to his feet and started toward the figure.

It turned toward him and spoke. "Hello, Galen. Why did you come back?"

Shocked, Galen automatically drew back the club in the darkness, then hesitated. "Reuben!" Galen exclaimed, keeping his voice low so that the Israelite sentries wouldn't hear him. "I didn't expect to see you!"

"I'm very late getting the water skins filled, and I'm very surprised to see you, too!"

"I see." Galen quickly lowered the club, hoping Reuben hadn't seen it.

Reuben apparently hadn't because he asked, "Didn't you get safely back to your camp last night?"

"Yes. I had to come back to . . . to . . ." He let his voice trail off.

Reuben prompted, "To what?"

"Uh . . ." Galen muttered, thinking fast. He could not tell Reuben that Goliath had instructed him to clout an Israelite and bring back some proof that he had hurt him. Yet in the same instant Galen felt the weight of the club in his hand and realized that this was his opportunity.

He could strike the unsuspecting boy before him, take something personal from his fallen body, and vanish back into the valley. It would take only seconds, then Galen could quietly return in triumph to show Goliath. That would earn the giant's respect, and prove that he could be a good Philistine soldier who would someday carry Goliath's shield ahead of him into battle.

But the thought of hitting Reuben sickened Galen. He knew that would be wrong.

"Well?" Reuben asked. "Why did you come back?"

"I . . . uh . . ." Galen stammered while his mind spun with possible excuses he might offer.

He told himself, *My tribe is threatening his people, but he and I aren't at war. It would be wrong to harm someone—especially Reuben—just to prove something to Goliath.*

Reuben stepped closer, saying, "What's the matter? Why can't you tell me?"

Galen didn't reply while his mind wildly plunged

on. *I feel so helpless! If I go back without doing something to an Israelite, Goliath will laugh at me! I'll never get to be a man and carry his shield! Besides, everyone else will think I'm a coward and I'll be disgraced forever!*

Reuben turned so that his face was faintly visible in the reflected light of the distant campfires. Smiling, he said, "You don't have to tell me if you don't want. We can just talk."

Galen nodded, greatly relieved at the reprieve. He knew his problem wasn't solved, but maybe he could think of a way to handle it. Still, he was so upset that he didn't feel like talking; he needed action.

"Or," he countered, realizing that instead of wanting to harm Reuben, he wanted to be friends, "we could have another play-fight."

"Too dark," Reuben replied. "We might hurt each other. But we could play war. One of us can hide while the other tries to find him. You know, like a spy sneaking up on a sentry. All right?"

Galen agreed. "You want to be the sentry or the spy?"

"Sentry," Reuben promptly replied.

"Good!" Galen replied. "Just stay away from the

campfire lights. I don't want anyone to see me."
Galen turned to face the valley's darkness, but listened to the soft rustling sounds as Reuben ran to
hide.

Galen was dismayed when another thought
popped into his head. *This would be the perfect opportunity to make Goliath proud of me! I could—*

"Stop it!" he muttered aloud. He silently added,
I couldn't do something so terrible!

A little voice inside his head taunted him, *Are
you sure? Maybe you'll change your mind! Isn't that
better than being thought of as a coward?* Galen
shook his head and began looking for Reuben.

———

Galen's nighttime search involved sneaking up
on bushes, large rocks, and a few trees where the
"sentry" might be watching for the infiltrating "spy."
Galen, trained to become a Philistine warrior from
his youngest years, had learned one way to find
someone in darkness.

He dropped down low to quickly scan the horizon. Against its faint light, he barely discerned
Reuben's form pressed up against a tree trunk.

Using all the stealth skills he had learned, Galen

furtively circled around in back of Reuben. Silent as a shadow, with the club in his hands, Galen stealthily rose up just behind the unsuspecting boy.

It would be so easy! Galen realized, then, disgusted with himself, he threw the club down.

The sound made Reuben jump and whirl around. "You're good, Galen!" he admitted with a nervous laugh. "I didn't hear or see you!"

Galen felt around in the darkness and retrieved his club. "Thanks, but I don't like this game. Let's just talk."

"Fine! You can give me some tips on how you sneaked up on me like that."

Galen headed toward the sound of the brook. "I'd rather talk about something else."

"Like what?"

Galen didn't answer until they were back beside the water skins where the murmur of running water helped to cover their voices. "Tell me about your family." It wasn't what Galen really wanted to know, but he didn't feel like coming out directly to say what he did want.

"I already told you just about everything, except I don't think I mentioned my parents adopting two little alien children after their mother and father were found dead near our camp."

Galen asked, "Why did they do that? And why did you bring me food instead of turning me in to your soldiers?"

"Well, a long, long time ago," Reuben began, "my people were slaves in Egypt. Our God led us out of slavery and gave us this land where we are now. In the Book of the Law, He told us that we were not to do wrong to a stranger because we had been strangers in Egypt."

Those were curious ideas to Galen. Dagon, his god, had never told anyone anything, as far as Galen knew. He asked Reuben, "Is that why you brought me food and didn't turn me in although our people are enemies?"

"Our God trusts us," Reuben explained, "and He welcomes anyone who trusts in Him. I did that with you."

"Oh!" Ashamed, Galen eased the club head to the ground and opened his fingers to let it fall. He heard a light splash where it landed in the brook.

Galen took several seconds to ponder something before he spoke again. "Can your God make men?"

Laughing softly, Reuben spoke with assurance. "Of course! He created everyone, including you and me, and He will help us both to grow up to be good men."

Galen turned those words over and over in his mind as he said good-bye to Reuben and started across the Valley of Elah under cover of darkness. He didn't know how he could explain to Goliath why he had not struck an Israelite and brought back proof.

Maybe Dagon . . . he started to think and lightly touched the carved image snuggled against his side. The national god of the Philistines had not ever given instructions to be nice to strangers. In fact, from what Galen knew, Dagon was primarily believed to be responsible for growing grain and other crops. How could a carved image help a boy become a real man?

Galen's thoughts were momentarily interrupted when he imagined what Goliath would say when he reported on his second experience inside Israelite lines. The thought scared him so that he suddenly shivered. He flinched as he visualized Goliath's fury turning from angry words to delivering powerful slaps with immense hands.

With an effort, Galen forced his mind back to the more pleasant thoughts about the God of

Reuben. Crossing the Valley of Elah under a star-splattered sky, Galen looked up. He wondered if Reuben's God was truly the most powerful of all gods, or even if there *were* any other gods.

Galen whispered, "The God of Reuben's people, if You are the only God, and I find that out that You have all power and might, I will follow You. And I want You to make me a man."

He paused, then added silently, *And I can't really wait until I grow up because tomorrow Goliath is going to make me wish I had never been born!*

CHAPTER 9

Passing out of the valley in the darkness, Galen approached his people's camp with sharply different feelings fighting inside him. A sense of peace over his decision was almost overwhelmed by the dread of facing Goliath. That reluctance and lack of courage made Galen fight to not run away in panic. Knowing he really had no choice, he answered the Philistine night sentry's challenge and entered the camp.

Galen didn't mention his adventure to the sentry, but walked through the sleeping encampment toward Ziklag's family tent. Glancing up at the midnight sky, he desperately wished his parents and his brother were alive so he could share the conflicts raging in his mind.

Hearing snoring from inside Zik's shelter, Galen removed his sandals to slip inside without awakening anyone. As he reached for the tent flap, Zik stepped outside.

He took Galen's arm, pulled him away from the tent, and demanded in a hoarse whisper, "Where have you been?"

Galen thought fast as they moved far enough away so that nobody could overhear. He had to talk to somebody, and he liked and trusted Zik. After swearing him to secrecy, Galen told him everything.

Zik sank down beside a dying campfire that made his face glow and his eyes shine brightly. He exclaimed in disbelief, "You talked to this God of the Israelites?"

"Well, sort of, I guess," Galen admitted, hurt that his confession seemed to have shocked Zik.

Galen watched the firelight playing on his friend's face before adding, "But I feel good about it." He touched the Dagon in his tunic. "And I also feel bad."

"But," Zik pointed out, "you can't even see this Israelite God, so how can you know what he thinks?"

"Well," Galen replied, "He left instructions in something called the Book of the Law."

"Tell that to Goliath!" Zik whispered. "Or are

you really going to tell him everything you've just told me?"

Thoughtfully, Galen admitted, "I don't think so. He's going to be angry enough that I had a chance to use my club on an Israelite but didn't."

Sighing heavily, Zik remarked, "I think you have lost all your chances with Goliath. I doubt that he'll ever, ever let you carry his shield. But you can be sure he's going to have something terrible to say about you becoming a man and a warrior. In fact, the whole camp probably will hear him when he curses you as only he can."

Galen shivered, recalling how vile-mouthed the giant had often been to anyone who aggravated him. It seemed to Galen that all he ever wanted was forever lost.

Zik continued, "You can see Dagon, Baal, and our other Philistine gods as easily as you can see Goliath. After all, he's the most powerful champion who ever was! My father says Goliath was sent by our Philistine gods to defeat the weak, foolish Israelites across the valley."

Galen protested rather lamely, "Reuben says that the God of the Israelites will defeat Goliath."

Zik laughed in derision. "Why would a powerful

God choose such cowardly people as the Israelites who won't even send one man to fight Goliath? Why would a powerful God give his people poor wooden weapons and no iron or bronze ones? It doesn't make sense!"

Zik's voice began to rise, but he ignored Galen's warning to speak softly. "Them defeat Goliath?" Zik cried. "That's impossible! For nearly 40 days, morning and evening, Goliath has challenged the Israelites to send somebody to fight him. No one has come."

Galen replied, "Reuben says that when it's the right time, their God will send someone to—"

"It won't happen!" Zik interrupted. "The Israelites won't ever send anyone to meet Goliath. They don't want to become our slaves when Goliath beats their champion. They sit over there on their hillside and shake with fear, but they won't fight! Some God they have!"

On that triumphant note, Zik declared that he was going to bed. Galen stayed outside to think, but he was now in more mental anguish and uncertainty than before. In spite of his determination to be a good Philistine, tears won. They continued for a long time. It was nearly dawn before he wearily crawled into the tent and slept.

He was awakened by Zik shaking him by the shoulders. "Wake up, Galen! Something seems to be happening on the Israelite side of the valley!"

Galen rolled over and muttered sleepily, "What?"

"You slept through Goliath's morning call for the Israelites to send someone to fight him. Today their soldiers are moving around excitedly instead of just standing around as usual."

Abruptly, Galen sat upright. "What does that mean?"

"Goliath thinks they may finally be going to send someone to fight him, so he's giving them a few minutes, then he's going to challenge them again! If he's right, there's going to be a wonderful sight to see! So get up!"

Galen quickly obeyed, wondering if Reuben could possibly be right about the Israelite God sending someone to accept Goliath's challenge.

Moments later, Galen and Zik pushed their way forward until they were past everyone except the

Philistine soldiers. Unable to see through the massed ranks, the boys ran off to one side. They stopped where there was a clear view of Goliath below them on the hillside and the Israelites on the opposite hill.

Zik spoke excitedly. "They're moving around like a swarm of bees, so they must have found a champion to fight ours! Do you suppose he's as big as Goliath?"

"I don't know," Galen admitted, feeling himself getting caught up in the excitement. He vainly looked for Reuben, and wondered if he could see him. "But," Galen told Zik, "whoever the Israelites plan to send against Goliath must really be a great warrior."

Galen dropped his gaze to his own people. As usual, the mighty Goliath and his shield bearer stood in front of his troops, facing the Israelites. Goliath made a splendid sight, towering more than nine feet tall in his 125-pound coat of scale armor. He looked even larger in his bronze helmet and greaves.

A bronze javelin was slung on his massive shoulders. At his side, a great sword rested in its scabbard. His spear, as large as a weaver's rod with a 15-

pound iron point, seemed tiny in Goliath's huge hands.

A few feet in front of him, Goliath's shield bearer waited, resting the giant's heavy buckler on the ground. Behind Goliath stood a warrior with a sword and spear. Galen had seen all the weapons in use before, and knew that the armor-bearer with the sword and spear was to follow Goliath and deliver a death blow after the giant felled an adversary.

None of that was different to Galen. Neither was the usual mass of Philistine warriors and civilians who had gathered morning and evening for forty days to see Goliath shout across the small valley for the Israelites to send out a champion to meet him in mortal combat.

What was different, Galen saw at once, was that on the hillside across the valley, the Israelites were no longer standing around with heads down and shoulders slumped. Instead, they ran back and forth, talking among themselves and often looking behind them.

Zik asked, "What do you think they see back there?"

"All I can see are officers' tents," Galen replied, shading his eyes to see better. "I think they're expecting someone to come from that direction. Yes! See? The troops are parting right in the middle, making room for someone to pass through them!"

"You're right!" Zik exclaimed. "Now I can hear them shouting something, but I can't make out their words."

"Neither can I," Galen admitted. "They're looking back and starting to cheer! Listen to them!"

A great roar erupted from the throats of the assembled Israelites. They shook their inferior bows and spears in the air and jumped up and down, straining to see whoever was moving through the human path behind them.

Zik cried, "No doubt about it! They've found a champion!"

"I see him!" Galen cried. "There! Just stepping out from—oh, no!"

He stared in disbelief. Across the valley, a boy not much older than Galen stepped out of the Israelites' ranks. He wore no armor, only shepherd's clothing. He carried a staff and sling, but no shield or weapon.

"Who's he?" Galen asked in surprise as the Israelites' cheers became a mighty and continuous roar.

"Probably a messenger," Zik guessed. "Maybe

he's being sent to say the Israelites have found a champion who needs a few more minutes to put on his armor. So this boy's going to ask if Goliath will wait."

Galen disagreed. "I don't think so. From the cheering of the Israelites and the way our warriors are laughing, I think that boy's going to challenge Goliath!"

"No! That can't be!" Zik declared emphatically.

Galen and Zik studied the youth with sudden new interest as he stopped at the brook and slowly picked up some stones from beside it.

He was a handsome lad, Galen had to admit. He was not as dark skinned as most Israelites. In fact, he had a ruddy complexion, and Galen thought from this distance the boy might even have red hair.

Galen watched as the youth bent to pick up a stone which he placed in the pouch of his shepherd's bag. Four times he repeated the action, then straightened up. Then, calmly and confidently, he left the stream and deliberately began walking toward Goliath.

"No!" Galen cried in disbelief. "*That* is their champion! That shepherd boy is going to fight Goliath with just a sling and some stones!"

CHAPTER 10

The Philistines also seemed to realize that this mere stripling of a youth was going to accept Goliath's challenge. His warriors laughed in contempt and shouted insults at the lone shepherd boy purposefully striding forward.

Zik exclaimed, "I just can't believe this! Those Israelites are actually sending a boy against Goliath!"

Galen breathlessly watched the handsome youth approach. He briefly wondered if Reuben was also watching this lad.

Galen told Zik, "I don't think Goliath believes it either. He probably feels insulted!"

When the opponents came within speaking distance, all cheering from the Israelite army and laughter from the Philistines slowly died down. The silence was broken only by the sound of Goliath's scale armor as he followed his shield bearer onto the valley floor.

Galen could not see the giant's face, but the sun shone directly on his youthful opponent's. Galen had a clear, sharp view of the handsome, ruddy shepherd. A beardless face proved that he was too young to be an experienced soldier.

He did not seem frightened; in fact, Galen thought the challenger appeared calm and confident although facing a warrior almost twice as tall as he.

Galen wished he knew the youth's name as the crowds on both sides of the valley became very quiet. Soon there was such a stillness that Galen could clearly hear Goliath's sneering words spoken to the youth.

"Am I a dog, that you come at me with sticks?"

Galen noticed the scorn and contempt in the giant's tone, and knew he despised the boy facing him. That was confirmed when Goliath began cursing the youth by the giant's gods of Dagon and Baal.

Zik whispered, "He's not even scaring that boy!"

Galen nodded, aware that the youthful stranger's countenance remained serene.

Goliath told him, "Come here, and I'll give your

flesh to the birds of the air and the beasts of the field."

The youth replied, "You come against me with sword and spear and javelin, but I come against you in the name of the Lord Almighty, the God of the armies of Israel, whom you have defied!"

Galen blinked, recalling how Reuben had said the Israelites' invisible God was going to send someone to defeat Goliath.

The shepherd continued, "This day the Lord will hand you over to me, and I'll strike you down and cut off your head! Today I will give the carcasses of the Philistine army to the birds of the air and the beasts of the earth, and the whole world will know that there is a God in Israel!"

Galen gasped, astonished that anyone dared to talk that way to Goliath, plus all the Philistine warriors.

The youthful challenger added, "All those gathered here will know that it is not by sword or spear that the Lord saves; for the battle is the Lord's, and He will give all of you into our hands!"

Galen watched Goliath move closer to attack the youth, who ran quickly to meet him.

Zik exclaimed, "I can't believe he's doing that!"

Galen didn't reply because he was intrigued by what the stranger did next.

He reached into his bag and took out one of the five stones he had picked up from the brook. Fitting the rock into the sling, the youth swung it rapidly above his head then released it.

Galen could barely follow its flight, but saw it clearly just before it struck the giant's forehead. Galen heard it hit; he saw the giant falter, then slowly topple like a great tree before an ax. Goliath crashed facedown on the ground.

Galen barely heard a collective cry of astonishment from the Philistines lined up on the hillside. Leaping back in shock, he cried aloud, "God of the Israelites, save me!"

He trembled with fear and excitement as the youth with the sling darted toward the fallen giant.

His shield bearer, standing in shock in front of Goliath, spun round and started running away, still carrying the great shield. As he drew even with Galen, he dropped it with a dull thud.

Galen's eyes flickered back to the stricken Goliath, and he again recalled Reuben's prophetic words about his God sending someone to overcome the giant.

Moments before, he had been a man nine feet tall, fully dressed head to toe in protective scale armor made of bronze. Now, sprawled facedown on the ground, he was still huge compared to the youth standing over him; yet somehow Goliath looked small and insignificant to Galen.

The victorious youth who had toppled the giant reached down and pulled big Goliath's sword from its scabbard. The sunlight glittered on the blade as he swung it high above Goliath's head. Galen quickly turned away and saw the looks of absolute disbelief on the Philistine warriors' faces.

They shrieked in a second collective howl of hysterical anguish as the sword flashed down. Instantly, Israelite soldiers triumphantly yelled and charged across the valley, brandishing mattocks, axes, and ox goads. A few had crude wooden spears or bows and arrows. Others carried slings.

The panicked Philistines turned and ran away from the onrushing hordes. Galen glanced toward Ziklag and saw him already frantically dashing after them.

Galen's mind told him to run for his life, but his feet would not obey. Terror had frozen him where he stood, trance-like, watching the swarm of

Hebrew soldiers surging across the narrow valley. They were covering the distance in an amazingly short time.

Galen's eyes were drawn back to the conquering shepherd boy as he lifted high his grisly trophy.

This horrific sight broke Galen's hypnotic trance. He turned and started to run after his fleeing tribesmen, but he had waited too long. He could not catch up with them.

Frantically looking around for somewhere to hide, he saw only one possibility: Goliath's great shield that his bearer had dropped in his flight.

Even though Galen had once struggled to lift it, fear gave him strength. With the dreaded shouts of the oncoming Israelites in his ears, Galen lifted an edge of the shield high enough to squirm headfirst under it.

Just before the shield fell protectively over him, he had a final glimpse of the foremost Israelites now rushing upon the scene.

Trembling in terror, Galen hoped no one could see him as he hid under Goliath's abandoned shield. His eyes quickly adjusted from the bright daylight to the semi-darkness under the shield. His drumming heart seemed as if it might burst through his ribs as he waited for the onrushing Israelites.

At first, he heard only their war cries and the fading shrieks of the terrorized Philistine warriors as they tried to escape the pursuing Israelites.

It had all happened so fast that Galen had a hard time believing what he had just seen. Goliath the giant was dead, brought down by a shepherd boy armed only with a sling and a stone. The witnessing Philistine soldiers were running away in panic. Galen had not dreamed that the Israelites with their inferior weapons would chase mighty warriors with their iron and bronze ones. But it was happening just as Reuben had predicted.

Galen heard the thud of countless running feet rushing toward his hiding place. The ground trembled where he lay facedown, helpless and alone. A dreadful thought exploded in his brain: *What if one of those Israelites stops and picks up this shield?*

The idea was so frightening that Galen cried out to the God of the shepherd boy; to the God of Reuben, the God whose name he did not know, but in whose power and might Galen now believed. "Save me!"

It was all he could think to do as the first wave of Israelite soldiers flowed around Goliath's fallen shield. Galen pressed his face against the earth and tried to hold his breath as the horde of victorious, shouting Israelites thundered past him.

He could hear the distinctive twang of bow-strings as they released their arrows at the fleeing Philistines. He caught the short grunt of exertion as Israelites hurled spears and javelins.

The shriek of wounded and dying men mingled with the noise of wooden spears being splintered by bronze and iron swords. This told Galen that hand-to-hand combat had begun between the foremost Israelites and the Philistine stragglers.

In a vain effort to shut out the awful clash of battle and shouts of victor and vanquished, Galen clapped both hands over his ears and prayed he would survive.

He didn't know how long he stayed that way, but gradually he became aware that the battle sounds were fading into the distance. He took both hands from his ears, cocked his head, and listened.

There was no doubt; the noise of battle was getting fainter as the Israelites hotly pursued the Philistines. Scarcely daring to believe he had been spared, he felt his racing pulse slow as apprehension ebbed away. For the first time, he thought of Zik and his other friends. Had they survived? Or were they sprawled out there on the bloody ground?

Slowly, carefully, with great effort, Galen eased the edge of Goliath's shield up and allowed a sliver of light into his shelter. The combatants had all vanished beyond a small hill, but dropped weapons and human casualties littered the area where the Philistine camp had been. The sight caused a wave of nausea to wash over Galen. He closed his eyes until the feeling passed.

Looking out again, his probing eyes showed nobody left standing. With a heavy sigh, Galen started to push up on the heavy shield so he could slide out, then stopped. Off to his right, where he had not looked before, two Israelite soldiers were heading straight toward his hiding place!

Galen sucked in his breath and dropped the edge of the shield. The welcoming soft darkness quickly engulfed him as his heart again started racing. He curled up in a tight little ball and suppressed a moan.

While the Israelite soldiers were still some distance away, Galen heard one speak in a deep voice.

"I can hardly wait to take whatever valuables Goliath has on him."

Galen swallowed hard as the two voices passed him some distance away. He heard the second soldier speak.

"I still don't think we should be doing this. We'll be in big trouble if our commander finds out we slipped away to strip the slain before the fight was over."

Galen noticed that this soldier spoke in a thin voice that suggested he might be a much younger man.

"Stop complaining!" the one with the deep voice growled. "Just be thankful we've got first pick of all these bronze and iron weapons. There! See that sword? Take it for yourself."

Galen had to strain to catch the other man's reply as both soldiers moved away from the fallen shield.

"Maybe I will. I can also use that bronze javelin over there, and that spear with the iron point."

His friend laughed. "You'll be so loaded down you'll hardly be able to walk. Remember, we have to carry it somewhere and hide it until it's safe to come back for it. I'm going to wait for whatever Goliath's got on him."

Galen strained hard to hear what else was said, but he guessed the men had come to where the giant had fallen. He heard the faint clink of Goliath's mail armor and the murmur of the scavengers' voices. Galen wondered if he dared try to slip away, but decided it was too risky. He could not outrun a thrown spear or an arrow.

Moments later, Galen regretted that decision when he heard the men walking back toward him. He began to tremble as they drew close enough for him to understand their words.

The younger man asked, "Where do you think we can hide all this for a while?"

"Over there looks like a good place."

Over where? Galen wondered, hoping they weren't going to come anywhere near him. But when the deep-voiced man spoke again, Galen knew his hope was in vain. The man was definitely coming toward where he was hiding.

The same man said, "We deserved getting first choice of these things because it's the only reward we'll get. Well, except for Goliath falling into our hands."

The younger man laughed. "*Our* hands? For 40 days, you and I stood and quaked with fright just as all the rest of our people did before David came along."

David? Galen thought from under the shield. *Could that be the name of the shepherd who killed Goliath?*

"That boy was a real surprise," the older man agreed with a chuckle. "You should have seen him when he came into camp with some roasted grain and loaves of bread for our commander. That was just shortly before Goliath shouted his usual challenge."

Galen licked his lips, realizing that the man's voice was now much closer than before. Galen guessed the men were slowly moving his way, still looting the slain. *They'll want Goliath's shield if they see it!* Galen thought, and his trembling increased. If the Israelites picked up the shield, would they strike him down, or make him a slave?

The younger man said doubtfully, "I heard that David had come to see his brothers who are in our unit."

"Yes, he did," the Israelite soldier answered. "I was standing near him when he greeted his brothers. That was when our people began shouting war cries and calling for us to form our lines facing Goliath, who had come out to taunt us."

"I wish I'd seen that part," the young soldier replied wistfully.

"If you had, you would never forget it," his comrade answered emphatically. "Goliath shouted as usual, and our men turned and ran from him in fear. Well, of course I didn't. I've seen too many battles to do that."

Galen listened in fascination, yet with dread because the Israelites were now definitely drawing closer to his hiding place.

The deep-voiced man continued, "David watched Goliath shout across the valley, then he turned to me and some others standing there. He asked who was this Philistine that he should defy the armies of the living God? Just at that moment, David's older brother Eliab walked up and heard him. He was angry and accused David of coming to see the battle."

"Is that when he was taken to see King Saul?"

"No, not right then, because David protested that wasn't why he had come. But someone overheard him and ran to tell Saul. I followed along and was present when David told the king that he would go and fight Goliath."

Galen cringed as the sound of footsteps neared. He swallowed hard and felt his mouth go dry with fear.

"So I heard," the younger soldier replied. "But is it true that finally Saul agreed, and put his own armor on David?"

"Oh, that's true. You know that Saul stands a head taller than all the rest of us, so it was really comical to see David trying to walk with all of Saul's armor, including his bronze helmet. Anyway, David took it all off and even handed back Saul's sword. Then he went down to the brook and picked up some stones."

"I saw him do that," the younger man declared.

"But why did he take five stones? He only needed one—"

Galen stiffened in alarm as the speaker suddenly broke off his sentence. *What happened?* he wondered.

"What're you looking at?" the man with the deep voice asked.

"That's Goliath's shield!" the younger soldier cried.

"It *was* his," his friend replied. "Now it's mine!"

Galen's skin crawled at the sound of a few hurried footsteps, then the sight of large fingers slipping under the edge of the shield just inches from his face!

G alen thought his heart would burst from sheer fright as the soldier's fingers started to lift the edge of Goliath's shield. Galen drew his feet under him in the vain hope that he might surprise the men so much he could jump up and run out of range of either an arrow or spear before they could react.

"Wait!" he heard the younger man exclaim. "I saw it first, so that shield is mine!"

The deep-voiced man angrily growled, "Who do you think you're telling what to do?"

"You, that's who! You took what you wanted from Goliath, so I got nothing! But I want his shield!"

He heard the older man growl, "So do I, so you can't have it! Now, leave me alone before—"

He broke off as Galen heard the distinctive sound of a sword being pulled from its scabbard.

The fingers disappeared from the edge of the shield. It fell heavily, again leaving Galen in semi-darkness. He caught the sound of a second sword being swiftly drawn from its scabbard.

The older man roared, "Pull a blade on me, will you? You fool! Now I'll take both the shield and your life!"

The ring of swords striking each other confirmed to Galen that the two soldiers were attacking each other. With furious shouts and loud panting, they pressed their assaults. Galen didn't know whether to crawl out from under the shield and try to run away, or wait to learn what happened.

He remained still, following the clash of the life-or-death struggle that surged back and forth around his hiding place. Slowly, numb with fright, Galen realized that the fight was moving away from him.

After taking a minute longer to be sure, with sudden hope he risked raising the edge of the great shield. The two men were so engrossed in their fight that all their attention was on each other.

Still, Galen hesitated, debating what to do. If he ran, they might see him, stop their combat, and bring him down with a javelin or arrow. But if he stayed hidden, what then? Surely the victor would come to claim the shield. He would be discovered, and a soldier who had just fought to the death with one of his own kind would surely not spare an enemy Philistine boy.

He took another rapid peek at the combatants. They had dropped their swords and were rolling around on the ground, too busy to notice him.

Once again Galen called out to Reuben's invisible God. "Save me!"

At the same time, he strained to lift the edge of Goliath's shield farthest away from the men. Frantic to escape, Galen wiggled out into the open and quickly got to his feet. Bending low, he ran awkwardly toward the darkening shadows of the Valley of Elah.

The shouting and cursing of the two combatants told Galen that they still had not seen him. He didn't look back, but felt his shoulder muscles tighten at the thought of an arrow striking him. He fled at his greatest possible speed across the valley toward the Israelite camp. Galen's lungs were on fire and his breathing was so tortured it came in rasping gasps before he decided he was out of bow-shot range.

He slowed his desperate pace and looked back. There were no shouts of anyone chasing him.

Greatly relieved, he took a moment to catch his breath. He had left one danger behind, but another loomed ahead.

Nervously, his eyes swept the Israelite camp. He was relieved to see that no soldiers had returned. There weren't even any young men, just old men and boys.

When none of them seemed to notice him, he started walking again. He was surprised that he staggered from exhaustion. He was aware of a painful stitch in his side that he had not noticed before. Cautiously, trying to control his suddenly wobbly legs, he walked on while his eyes flickered ahead in hopes of seeing Reuben.

Galen encouraged himself by thinking, *If I can just reach him, I'll be all right. I'll ask him to go with me to his parents. He said they had taken in other orphans; maybe they'll take me in too. I'll work hard for—*

He was jerked out of his musings by a shout from the Israelite camp. "Philistine! Philistine coming!"

A boy pointed toward him, screaming his warning over and over. Other boys ran to see too. They joined in shouting, "Philistine!"

In moments, a crowd had almost miraculously formed, facing him. A few older boys arrived late and pushed their way to the front of the crowd. These teenagers were armed with sticks, stones, and slings. Some elderly men, moving slowly with age, arrived with farmers' sickles, forks, and axes.

Now so exhausted that he could barely stay on his feet, Galen lurched toward the Israelites. They were silent, their faces grim as they gripped their stones and weapons.

Galen frantically scanned the growing crowd for Reuben, but didn't see him. Intimidated, he hesitated, his hands dropping wearily to his sides.

In his excitement, he had forgotten the image of Dagon carried in his tunic. Plunging his hand inside, Galen held up the carving of the Philistines' national deity. For a moment, he studied the carving of half-man, half-fish, and recalled Reuben's laughing remarks when he had first seen it by the brook.

That's Dagon? That silly little thing is your god you think can help you?

The words silently echoed in Galen's memory, along with what Reuben had said about the God of the Israelites sending someone to defeat Goliath.

Reuben was right, Galen admitted to himself. He

gazed thoughtfully down at Dagon's image. This visible Philistine god had not helped him, not a bit. Abruptly, mustering his remaining strength, Galen drew back his arm and hurled the object back into the Valley of Elah.

Raising his eyes to the sky, Galen confessed his fears and hopes to Reuben's invisible but powerful God who had sent a shepherd boy to overcome Goliath.

Galen whispered hoarsely, "Reuben's God, hear me! I am afraid these people lined up over there will kill me because I am a Philistine, but I have no place else to go! I was wrong about Dagon, and Reuben was right. You are the true source of power!"

Pausing, Galen fervently added, "It doesn't matter anymore that Goliath thought I was not strong, or that he would never be proud of me. It doesn't matter that I could not even lift his shield off the ground. Now I know that carrying Goliath's shield and killing people are not what make a man, but what he is inside. You used Reuben, a boy like me, to show that You are the only True God. If You're willing to use me, I'm ready and I'm willing. I want to be in Your family; to serve You and grow up to be a man that You'll be proud of! But I can't if these people stone me! I need help!"

A voice called from the crowd of Israelites, "Galen? Is that you?"

"Reuben!" Galen joyfully exclaimed, and forced his weary legs to run toward the hill.

Reuben raced to meet him, threw his arms around him, and exclaimed with a happy grin, "Welcome, Galen!"

Galen's weariness seemed to melt away in his joyous reunion. He thumped Reuben on the back and fought back tears of happiness. He couldn't stop the tremor in his voice as he blurted out his thoughts from a full heart.

"I've never been so glad to see anyone in my life! I threw away Dagon and asked your God to let me serve Him! I want to be a part of His family.

"I was afraid of those people watching me, but I told your God that I trusted Him because you said He would send someone to overcome Goliath. So now I can't go back over there," he pointed across the Valley of Elah. "I have no one but you to turn to!"

Reuben grinned and grabbed Galen's arm, saying, "Come with me." He turned away, pulling on Galen.

"Where're we going?" Galen asked, glancing dubiously at the Israelites watching them as the boys moved through the camp.

Over his shoulder, Reuben explained, "To see my father. He'll welcome you—and so will my mother when we get home."

Galen exclaimed, "Really?"

Reuben stopped and smiled reassuringly. "Really!"

Staring, Galen cried, "You mean, you think they'll take me in and give me a real home?"

Reuben's arm slid across Galen's shoulders. "I know they will. Not only that—you'll be my brother!"

Happily laughing, the boys broke into a run.

Letters From Our Readers

Where can I find this story in the Bible?

Lauren Styles, Anderson, IN

You can find the story of David and Goliath in 1 Samuel 17. You won't find any mention of Galen or Reuben, though. When we hear the Bible story in Sunday school, we see the events from the Israelites' point of view. But the author wondered how a Philistine would see the story. What would it be like for a Philistine boy to see his people's hero defeated by an Israelite teen not much older than himself? And what would happen if this boy realized that his Philistine god Dagon could not help him? How could he learn about the One True God?

That's why the author imagined the boys Galen and Reuben—to help you see what it was like to live then and watch this amazing event in Israel's history. Of course, while the part about Galen, Reuben, and the other boys is imagined, the part about David, Goliath, King Saul, and the armies is true.

Who were the Philistines and where did they come from?

Jon Emerson, Tallahassee, FL

The Philistines were a people from the area around the Aegean Sea or perhaps from the island of Crete (nobody knows for sure). They settled along the coast of Canaan before the time of Abraham. If you look at a map in your Bible, you can locate some major Philistine cities that are mentioned in the story: Gaza, Ashkelon, Ashdod, Gath, and Ekron. (Look west of Jerusalem, along the coast of the Great Sea.)

The Philistines manufactured iron tools and weapons, which gave them military superiority over the Israelites. They were at the height of their power during the reigns of King Saul (when this story takes place) and King David. After a while, though, their civilization disappeared.

Why did the Philistines worship a god carved out of wood or stone? Didn't they know it didn't have any power to help them?

Justin Vanderwel, Kansas City, KS

There's a yearning in every person's heart to know God, and if people cannot find the One True God, they will create a substitute. (Sometimes people know about the One True God, but refuse to follow Him.)

The Bible is filled with stories about people who worshiped false gods (called heathens), as well as stern warnings to the Israelites to stay away from heathen religions. But even King Solomon, a man to whom God granted great wisdom, was enticed by false gods through his heathen wives (see 1 Kings 11:1–3).

Today, people are still worshiping false gods. If you look around at our culture, you'll see evidence of this every day. But the Bible still warns us to have nothing to do with heathen religions or idols (1 John 5:21; 1 Corinthians 10:14; Leviticus 26:1).

Why were there women and children in the Philistine camp in this story?

Emma Clark, Cookeville, TN

Some reference books say that the Philistines took their families along when they went to war. The families remained in camp, while the men went into battle. Although the Israelites didn't do this, David's father did send him to take food and bring back a report about his older brothers (see 1 Samuel 17:17–18).

Was Goliath *really* over nine feet tall?

Randy Jackson, Pocatello, ID

Yes! No wonder the Israelites didn't want to fight him. Not only was he much larger than any of the Israelite soldiers, but he also had better armor and weapons. (See 1 Samuel 17:4–7 for a description of Goliath and his armor.) But David wasn't fighting Goliath in his own strength—he knew that only God could defeat Goliath. He made sure everyone understood that God would help him win the battle against the giant (1 Samuel 17:45–47).

PRINCIPLES *and* PRACTICE *of*

Interventional
Cardiology